Other books by Mick Inkpen:

KIPPER

KIPPER'S BIRTHDAY

ONE BEAR AT BEDTIME

THE BLUE BALLOON

THREADBEAR

BILLY'S BEETLE

PENGUIN SMALL

LULLABYHULLABALLOO !

WHERE, OH WHERE, IS KIPPER'S BEAR ?

British Library Cataloguing in Publication Data

Inkpen, Mick
Kipper's toybox.
I. Title
823.914 [J]

ISBN 0-340-56081-9

First published 1992
10 9 8 7 6 5 4 3

Published by Hodder Children's Books,
a division of Hodder Headline plc,
338 Euston Road, London NW1 3BH

Printed in Singapore Through Printlink International Co

Kipper's Toybox

Mick Inkpen

Hodder
Children's
Books

a division of Hodder Headline plc

Someone or something had been nibbling a hole in Kipper's toybox.

'I hope my toys are safe,' said Kipper. He emptied them out and counted them.

'One, two, three, four, five, six, SEVEN! That's wrong!' he said. 'There should only be six!'

Kipper counted his toys again.
This time he lined them up to
make it easier.

   'Big Owl one, Hippopotamus two,
Sock Thing three, Slipper four,
Rabbit five, Mr Snake six.

   'That's better!' he said.

Kipper put his toys back in the toybox. Then he counted them one more time. Just to make sure.

'One, two, three, four, five, six, seven, EIGHT NOSES! That's two too many noses!' said Kipper.

Kipper grabbed Big Owl and
threw him out of the toybox.
'ONE!' he said crossly.
Out went Hippopotamus, 'TWO!'
Out went Rabbit, 'THREE!'
Out went Mr Snake, 'FOUR!'
Out went Slipper, 'FIVE!'
But where was six? Where was
Sock Thing?

Kipper was upset. Next to Rabbit,
Sock Thing was his favourite.
Now he was gone.

'I won't lose any more of you,'
said Kipper. He picked up the rest of
his toys and put them in his basket.
Then he climbed in and kept watch
until bedtime.

That night Kipper was woken by a strange noise.

It was coming from the corner of the room.

Kipper turned on the light. There, wriggling across the floor, was Sock Thing! It must have been Sock Thing who had been eating his toybox!

Kipper was not sure what to do. None of his toys had ever come to life before. He jumped back in his basket and hid behind Big Owl.

Sock Thing wriggled slowly round in a circle and bumped into the basket. Then he began to wriggle back the way he had come.

He did not seem to know where he was going. Kipper followed.

Quickly Kipper grabbed him
by the nose. Sock Thing squeaked
and wriggled harder.

Then a little tail appeared.
A little pink tail.

And a little voice said,
'Don't hurt him!'

'So it was YOU! You have been making the hole in my toybox!' said Kipper.

It was true. The mice had been nibbling pieces of Kipper's toybox to make their nest.

'You must promise not to nibble it again,' said Kipper.

'We promise,' said the mice.

In return Kipper let the mice share his basket. It was much cosier than a nest made of cardboard and the two little mice never nibbled Kipper's toybox again...

But their babies did.
They nibbled EVERYTHING!